SOCCER
GIRLS ROCKING IT

NICHOLAS FAULKNER and JOSEPHA SHERMAN

ROSEN PUBLISHING

NEW YORK

Published in 2016 by The Rosen Publishing Group, Inc.
29 East 21st Street, New York, NY 10010

First Edition

Library of Congress Cataloging-in-Publication Data

Faulkner, Nicholas.
 Soccer : girls rocking it / Nicholas Faulkner and Josepha Sherman. – First Edition.
     pages cm. – ((Title IX Rocks! Play Like a Girl))
 Includes index.
 ISBN 978-1-5081-7039-6 (Library bound)
 1. Soccer for girls–Juvenile literature. I. Sherman, Josepha. II. Title.
 GV944.5.F38 2016
 796.334082–dc23
                                        2015018391

Manufactured in China

CONTENTS

Soccer, also known as football around the world, is one of the oldest sports. It is also one of the most popular, with millions worldwide gathering to watch the World Cup. Its popularity comes from the fact that almost anyone can play it. You just need the physical ability, the passion, some teammates, and any empty lot or field. With that, you have the makings of a soccer match.

And this game isn't just for the boys. Modern women's soccer has gained tremendous popularity in recent years, with the USA winning the Women's World Cup in 2015, but it has also been around for quite a while. The first recorded women's soccer games occurred in the late nineteenth century. Then, in the late 1960s and early 1970s, women's soccer associations started to form in the UK. Women's soccer has also been an Olympic event since 1996.

But there's more to the sport than just worldwide fame. Soccer brings people together. All different types of people come together to enjoy playing or watching the game. Also, the sport helps you develop as a person. It teaches discipline, self-respect, and respect for others, including your opponents, regardless of what gender you are.

In 1972, the US Congress passed the Education Amendments. Title IX, part of the Education Amendments, says: "No person in the United States shall, on the basis of sex, be excluded from participation in, be denied the benefits of, or be subjected to discrimination under any

Cathura Ramoi, goalie of Papua New Guinea's team in the Girls' Youth Olympic Football Tournament, fails to save a shot by Dilan Akarsu of Turkey.

education program or activity receiving federal financial assistance." In the past, sports programs and scholarships in schools were geared mostly to boys and young men. Now, though, all that's changed. Under Title IX, high schools and colleges must offer young women the same opportunities as young men. For the sport of soccer, this is especially good news since it is a game for everyone, not just the boys.

According to the Women's Sports Federation, there are a number of reasons for girls to get involved in soccer. Young women athletes are three times as likely to graduate as those who don't play sports. Soccer, and sports in general, tends to boost one's confidence, which is especially important during the challenging adolescent and high school years. Also, young athletes are more likely to get involved in leadership positions, such as student government. With all the advantages that sports can offer young women, why not get involved? With that said, let's learn a little about soccer.

CHAPTER ONE

SOCCER BASICS

So where did soccer come from? That's a question no one has been able to answer. Some people claim that the game started in ancient Egypt or in ancient China, where games closely related to soccer were being played over two thousand years ago. Others point to the ancient Romans, who played a game called *harpastum*, which may have been an ancestor of soccer. And in the New World, Native American tribes in New England played a game called *pasuckquakkohowog*, which means "gathering to play ball with the foot."

Some form of soccer was played in the American colonies as early as the settling of Jamestown in 1609, but the game was banned as a "bad influence" and nearly disappeared over the next two centuries.

But the sport as we know it today dates to 1863, when the London Football Association set down the first rules. Soccer came to the United States with British immigrants in the middle of the nineteenth century, but at first no one was really very interested in it. The sport didn't become widely known until 1908, when soccer became an Olympic event. Even so, soccer didn't really catch on in the United States until the 1970s, when a champion Brazilian soccer player named Pelé became an international superstar. After that, soccer began to be played in schools and sports clubs. It was not until 1996, however, that soccer became an Olympic event for women. In that first year of women's competition, the United States captured the gold medal.

Soccer is among the most popular sports in the world, but not everyone knows the rules. The short version is, one team tries to score points by getting a soccer ball into the other team's goal while preventing the other team from scoring on its goal.

What makes soccer different from any other game is the fact that, except for the goalkeeper, players are not allowed to use their hands or arms. Instead, they can move and touch the ball with any other part of their bodies, such as their feet, thighs, chest, and even their heads! A soccer game has one referee, who has two assistants, called linespeople, who make sure that all the rules of the game are obeyed.

ON THE FIELD

Soccer fields don't have a set size, although they are always rectangular and grassy. They are usually between 100 and 130 yards (91 and 119 meters) long and anywhere from 50 to 100 yards (46 to 91 meters) wide. The two goalposts are set on the short sides of the rectangle, with goal lines drawn in front of them. Each goalpost is made of two upright poles and a crossbar, backed by what looks like a big box made of net, open on the field side.

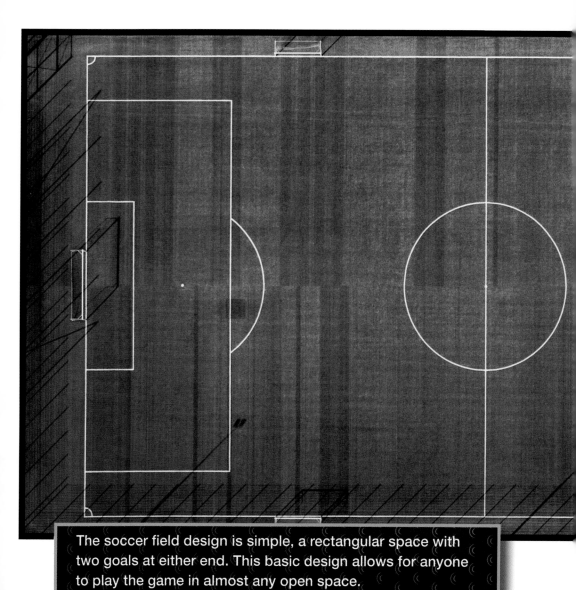

The soccer field design is simple, a rectangular space with two goals at either end. This basic design allows for anyone to play the game in almost any open space.

In front of each goal is the penalty area, 18 yards (16 m) long and 44 yards (40 m) wide. This is the only place where the goal-keeper can use her hands. If she ventures out of the penalty area, she must use only her feet, legs, chest, and head like everyone else. The benches, the area for coaches and substitute players, are

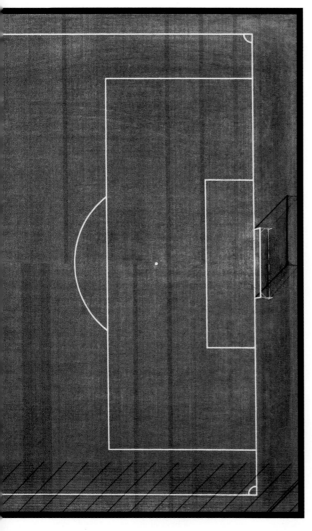

on the two longer sides, just outside the sidelines.

YOUR TEAMMATES

A soccer team usually has eleven players, although a beginning team or a very young team just learning the game might play with as few as five on the field at one time. Ten of the eleven players are field players and try to score goals, or keep the other team from stealing the ball and getting in a position to shoot on their net. The ten are divided into three areas: forwards, midfielders, and defenders.

Forwards are a team's offense. They are the players who drive the ball forward and try to score. They also must be ready to help the midfielders and defenders get the ball from the other team.

Midfielders, who are midway between offense and defense, are perhaps the hardest working players on a team. They need to play both roles in a game and offer support to the forwards and defenders. They are constantly on the move, running upfield to help the

The United States women's national soccer team won the FIFA Women's World Cup against Japan on July 5, 2015. The US team scored four goals in the game's first sixteen minutes.

forwards score or running back to assist the defenders in preventing the other team's offense from taking a shot on their goal.

Defenders, as the name implies, defend, stopping the other team from scoring and getting the ball away from opponents whenever they can. They are often the ones who begin an attack toward the opponent's goal by stealing the ball and passing it to a midfielder.

The eleventh player on the team is called the goalkeeper or goalie. She stands in front of the goal, and her job is to keep the other team from scoring. She can do this by grabbing the ball or stopping it with her body before it can go through the goalposts. She then throws or punts it back onto the field away from the goal. Some goalies make truly amazing jumps and dives to block a ball.

THE RULES OF THE GAME

A soccer game begins with a coin toss. The winner of the toss gets to decide which goal it will defend; the other team gets the ball first. At kickoff, one player passes to her teammate at the center of the field, putting the ball in play. Players can move the ball in any direction and can pass the ball back and forth to each other as often as they like, as long as they're not offside. Being offside is when an offensive player who doesn't have the ball is closer to the opponent's goal line than all but one opponent (usually the goalie). Allowing a player to be offside would make scoring too easy and give offense an unfair advantage.

Play continues until a goal is scored, the ball goes out of bounds over the sidelines or endlines, or there's a foul. When the ball does go out of bounds, the team that touched it last before it went out has to give up control of it. The other team gets a throw-in, which is a chance to throw the ball back onto the field from the sideline closest to where the ball went out. The throw-in can go anywhere on the field, but it can't score a goal. As for fouls, players can stop their opponents or steal the ball, but they can't deliberately push, trip, or hold them. A game lasts ninety minutes (although coaches with young players may decide on shorter games) with a brief half-time after forty-five minutes.

WHAT ARE FOULS?

The worst fouls in soccer are deliberately pushing, hitting, kicking, tripping, holding (hanging onto an opposing player), and charging a player from behind. The referee who calls any of these fouls gives the ball to the other team for one direct free kick. With a direct free kick, a member of the team that has been fouled lines the ball up at the site of the penalty, takes a shot on the goal (if possible), or kicks it to a teammate.

Other fouls include use of hands or arms to control the ball, or obstructing play. The opposing team is given the ball for one indirect free kick. This means that the kick can't score a goal; the ball is lined up where the foul occurred and has to be passed at least once before a shot on goal can be made.

GET IN GEAR

Soccer isn't very expensive to play. But like any other sport, it does require certain gear.

Soccer players usually wear shorts and jerseys. If you're just playing with friends, any comfortable clothing that lets you move freely is good enough. If you're on a team, though, you'll wear a jersey in the team colors, with a number and the team name on it. Some teams are given their uniforms at their first meeting.

A soccer player wears cleats, plastic spiked sneakers that dig

A QUARTER CENTURY OF SOCCER IN THE STREETS

Over a quarter century ago in 1989, Carolyn McKenzie founded Soccer in the Streets to bring soccer and educational programs to inner-city young people. By 1999, one hundred thousand disadvantaged boys and girls had participated in the program. But not enough girls were joining. As a result, in 1999, the Urban Soccer Girl Program was formed. In 2000, the Positive Choice mentoring program was created so that soccer players, other athletes, and coaches could teach and encourage inner-city youngsters. Soccer in the Streets represented the United States at the Football for Hope Festival during the 2010 FIFA World Cup. In 2011, the organization won its first ATL Champions League.

Though soccer doesn't require much gear, the equipment is important. Proper cleats ensure a firm step on the grass, and shin guards protect the lower legs from injury.

into the grass and prevent slipping. But cleats can be dangerous for a beginning player who is not used to them; she could easily catch one in the ground and possibly sprain or twist an ankle. There's also a danger of accidentally stepping on another player's foot when running or on her body if she suddenly falls in front of you. If you're just playing for fun, any shoes that give you good footing on grass and good support for your ankles will do.

Guarding Yourself

This is the only part of your soccer clothing you'll need to buy in a sports store with a separate soccer department. Shin guards are made of cloth and plastic and fit over a player's shins—the front of her legs below the knees. It's important to get shin guards that fit properly; some can even be form fitted to your leg. Be sure to try on several pairs, and make sure they fit snugly and comfortably onto your legs. You'll also want a pair of soccer socks, which must be pulled up to cover your shin guards.

Protecting Your Hands

Generally, only the goalkeeper wears gloves. These are usually made of sturdy leather to protect her hands when she catches, stops, or throws the soccer ball. If you're going to be a goalie, be sure that your gloves are comfortably snug, allowing you to move your hands and each finger freely. Gloves that are too big get in the way when you're trying to catch or block a ball, and gloves that are too small can actually cut off circulation. This will lessen the feeling in your hands, making it much harder to catch and throw the ball.

The Soccer Ball

Soccer balls come in several sizes, from three, which is the smallest and used by the youngest players, up to five, which is the professional

Though there are soccer balls designed for professional use, you can use almost any ball to play the game. What's important is that it's light, durable, and the proper size.

size. Size five is approximately twenty-eight inches (seventy-one centimeters) in circumference (the width of the widest part of the ball) and weighs about one pound (sixteen ounces). There isn't any rule about material, but a soccer ball is usually made of leather or

rubber. A school team or soccer club will provide a soccer ball, but you may want to have your own so you can play and practice at home. The size of the soccer ball you use usually depends upon your age. Players who are eight years old or younger should use a size three, players who are nine to eleven years old should use a size four, and players twelve years old or older should use a size five.

CHAPTER TWO

TRAINING FOR SUCCESS

As the saying goes, practice makes perfect. This is especially true in soccer where skill is only part of the formula for success. But practice shouldn't be dull and boring.

If you play soccer, you're likely to get your share of bruises and scrapes, just as you would in any other sport. As long as you keep yourself in good shape and wear the proper equipment, you're not likely to suffer a serious injury—particularly if you're also careful to warm up and stretch your muscles before every game or practice session. It's important to get into a warm-up routine, doing the same exercises and stretches before each game. A warm-up session should last at least fifteen minutes.

In soccer, there are no shortcuts. To be successful, you must establish a training routine. Find a little time every day to exercise and practice soccer drills.

WARM UP TO PLAY SAFELY

Easy ways to warm up include jogging, skipping, and running with the ball. After your muscles are warmed up, stretch gently and slowly, working each part of the body in turn. As you get warmed up and stretched, you can start to move at faster speeds.

What types of injuries do soccer players suffer? The most common are bruises from getting kicked or hit by the ball. Another common injury is blisters to players' feet. Blisters can be avoided by getting shoes that fit properly and by taking time to break them in. Pulled or sore muscles are also common and can be prevented by proper warm-ups and enough rest between games and practice sessions.

More serious damage can happen to the joints of the knees and ankles. Because of soccer's quick starts, stops, and turns, a player can sprain or twist these joints, or injure them through repeated stress on specific areas. The causes of these injuries range from insufficient warm-up time and fitness to bad field conditions, such as holes or patches of mud. You can take care of the first problem yourself by warming up properly. The second problem should be reported to the coach or referee.

In addition, some younger players may suffer from Sever's disease, although the incidence of this is low. It isn't actually a disease; it is an injury to the heel. As young players undergo growth spurts, the lower leg bones grow faster than the tendons. This causes tension where the heel bone is attached to the Achilles tendon. Wearing worn-out shoes or rundown cleats can add to this tension, causing pain in the heels. Sever's disease can be treated with stretching exercises, but to avoid it, make sure you wear properly fitting shoes in good condition.

Another problem related to injury—one that can actually be a cause of injury—is too much training. Your coach might want you to be so fit that he or she makes you work out too hard or for too long. Or you might want to improve or win so badly that you push your body too far and don't let yourself rest. If your body doesn't have a chance to rest, it can't recover from the stresses you're putting on it. It gets weaker, not stronger. You play worse, not better. You get annoyed at yourself and play even harder. That, of course, only adds to the problem. You can easily end up with an injury or just burn out and not want to play soccer anymore. Make sure that your

Stretching is one of the most important things you can do to prevent injury. You should do a full body stretch before and after every time you play, including practice.

A FEW GAMES TO WARM UP

The best way to get good at a sport is to practice a lot, so you should try to make practice fun. Turn your practice exercises into a game. Here are a few to try.

The Circle Dribble: You need about ten players for this one, plus someone to act as signaler. Each player has a soccer ball. Stand in a circle and start dribbling the balls around the circle, with everyone moving in the same direction. Every time the designated player signals, everyone must immediately begin dribbling in the opposite direction, maintaining control of the ball. Since no one knows when the signal is coming, this isn't as easy as it seems!

Queen of the Circle: This is another game for about ten players. Each player has a soccer ball. At a signal, they all start dribbling the balls within a circle marked with chalk, string, or plastic pylons. As each player dribbles her ball, she also tries to kick other girls' balls out of the circle. The last player still dribbling her ball in the circle is the Queen of the Circle.

Goal Wars: Goalkeepers need to have fun, too, especially considering all the pressure they're under! Here's a game for two goalies. You set up two goals, placed about twenty feet (six meters) apart. One goalkeeper guards each goal. Both goalkeepers have soccer balls. Their aim is to score goals against

continued from page 22

each other as quickly as possible by throwing or kicking the ball into the other goalkeeper's goal. The first goalkeeper to score twenty goals wins.

training is balanced with enough rest and proper nutrition to help you avoid overtraining and its effects on your body.

EATING RIGHT

As you are getting ready for a game, you may feel the need for a quick energy boost. Maybe you snack on candy or drink a soda or two. That's not a good idea. The quick boost you get from sugar won't last long enough to help, and neither will the caffeine in the sodas. In fact, both caffeine and sugar leave you feeling more tired than you were before the brief burst of energy they provide. You might even get an upset stomach from the carbonation!

Instead, you're better off eating balanced meals every day, including protein (which is found in beans, tofu, fish, and chicken), fruits, vegetables, and grains. Some players like to eat pre-competition snacks and meals that are made up mostly of carbohydrates, such as pasta or high-energy nutrition bars, which can give you longer-lasting energy. Check with your doctor if you're not sure what diet is right for you.

Don't skip breakfast on the day of a game. You need to start off with the good, steady level of energy that only a proper meal can provide. You also don't want to eat too heavily just before playing;

this will make you sluggish and could lead to cramping. Try to eat at least three hours before it starts. But you do want to make sure that you get enough water before, during, and after the game. It's very easy to become dehydrated when you're active and not even realize it until you feel woozy. After the game, try to eat within an hour or two. Your body needs to refuel after using up so much energy.

KEEPING FIT

A good fitness program for soccer players should be well-rounded. Soccer is a demanding game that requires a lot of energy and a fair amount of skill. You will need to build up your endurance through running and your agility through a series of exercises and games, some of which were described earlier in this chapter.

You'll want to include strength training exercises as well. These exercises are very helpful, both in building up your strength and in giving you greater stamina, which will enable you to continue to play hard even in the last moments of a long, tiring game. Strength training, which includes lifting weights, will not necessarily give you bulging muscles. A good strength training program will give you a strong body, not an overly muscular one.

Your coach will probably set up your fitness program for you

Keeping fit involves cardio, or any exercise that increases your heart rate. Cardio exercises include running with the soccer ball, doing jumping jacks, or just simple light jogging.

and the rest of your team. If you want to create your own fitness program, ask your doctor for advice first.

CHAPTER THREE

HONING YOUR SKILLS

The beauty of soccer is that almost anyone can play the game in almost any location, whether it's in their backyards, on school teams, or in Olympic competition. It is also a game that requires skill and technique. Very few players are so naturally gifted that they can immediately master the most important soccer skills— dribbling, shooting, heading, passing, receiving, and goaltending. Each skill requires a lot of practice, and even the best players can always work to improve their skills.

THE DRIBBLE

You may think of basketball when you hear this term. Dribbling in soccer is similar, though it requires different parts of the body. In both games, the point of dribbling is to move the ball forward, but keep it under control so it can't be stolen by the other team.

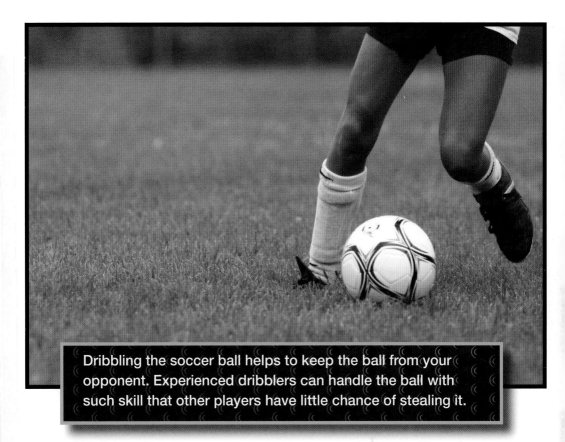

Dribbling the soccer ball helps to keep the ball from your opponent. Experienced dribblers can handle the ball with such skill that other players have little chance of stealing it.

Dribbling allows you to keep the ball until you can either pass it off to a teammate or take a shot on goal. But in soccer, unlike basketball, the ball is kept moving only with the feet, using small touches forward and to the side.

The way to dribble in soccer is to run with the ball, moving it forward carefully with tiny, controlled kicks. If your foot touches it too hard, the ball gets away from you. If you don't touch it hard enough, the ball gets caught under your feet and you might trip over the ball! You're working your way with the lightest touches you can manage. You also have to watch out for players on the other team who may try to steal the ball from you.

A good way to practice dribbling is just to run with the ball until you find your running rhythm and can touch the ball every other stride. Then try dribbling the ball at different speeds, slow to fast and back again. It's a good idea to be able to change speeds and directions during a game. You can fake out players from the other team that way. Try not to look only at the ball. It's important to keep your head up so you know where other players are. Practice this by spending less time looking at the ball while you're dribbling. With enough practice, you'll start to develop a sense of where the ball is without always having to look down.

TAKING THE SHOT

Shooting means kicking the ball to score a goal. To score, you need both power and accuracy to direct the ball where you want it to go with the inside, outside, or instep of your foot. (The instep is the top of the foot where your shoelaces are.)

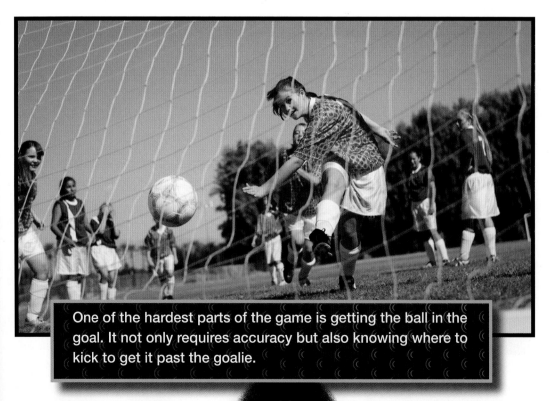

One of the hardest parts of the game is getting the ball in the goal. It not only requires accuracy but also knowing where to kick to get it past the goalie.

To practice, begin by shooting a motionless ball. As you become more accurate, practice shooting a rolling ball. Once you're pretty good at that, it's time to practice dribbling and shooting. You particularly want to try shooting low and hard. Low shots have a far better chance of scoring than high shots because they tend to be quicker and have more power behind them. High

THE PASSING GAME

As exciting as scoring a point for your team is, don't expect to score every goal all by yourself. That would be impossible. Remember, soccer is a team sport. Your teammates deserve a chance to score, too. The more people who can score on a team, the more dangerous your team is to the opposition. If you have the ball, but a teammate is in a better position than you to score, you should pass it to her. One of the most important skills you need to learn if you're to be a successful member of the team is how to pass and receive the ball.

There are several kinds of passes. Whichever one you choose, always remember to be careful where and when to pass. If there are too many members of the other team surrounding you, pass the ball to a teammate who has more space. Don't pass wildly at the first teammate you see just to get rid of the ball. Make sure she has a chance to receive it. If it looks like she's marked, or defended, don't pass it to her.

shots tend to lose their speed as they arc toward the goal, so they are easier to catch or block.

Look for the open space in the goal. Only look down at the ball just before you shoot. When you do shoot, keep watching your shot in case the ball hits a goalpost or the goalie and bounces back to you.

A good drill for sharpening your shooting accuracy is to kick a ball against a wall. Mark a target on the wall, back up about 10 feet (3 m), and shoot the ball at the target. Practice this every day, at least twenty kicks with each foot, until you can hit the target consistently. Next, back up to about 15 feet (4.5 m) away from the target and repeat. Then try shooting from 20 feet (6 m) away. Practice until you can hit the target at any range and from any direction. Practice using each foot. You may not always be in a position during a game to shoot from your right foot, but you may still be able to score a goal with your left foot.

You can also use the wall as a second "player." Throw the ball at the wall so that the ball bounces back to you, and try to shoot the ball back at the target. It's important to be able to shoot both a rolling ball and a bouncing ball. Practice until you can hit the target almost every time.

USING THE INSIDE OF YOUR FOOT

This is the easiest pass to learn, and it is also the most accurate. You place the foot you're not going to kick with at the side of the ball. You then kick the ball with the inside of your other foot. Be sure to hit the middle of the ball, not the side or bottom—otherwise the ball might not go where you are aiming it. Be sure that your ankle is locked, or stiff, so that your foot stays in the same direction all the way through the kick, aiming your foot in the direction that you want

Kicking the ball with the inside of the foot gives you the most accuracy. As a result, it is the most common way to pass the ball.

the ball to go. Follow through with the kick until your foot won't go any higher.

As with the shooting exercises, you can practice this pass using a wall and a target. Don't worry if you can't hit the ball very far: This pass is for accuracy, not power.

USING THE OUTSIDE OF YOUR FOOT

As you can tell from the name of this pass, it is similar to the inside-the-foot pass. Instead of kicking with the inside of your foot, however, you kick the ball with the outside of your foot, making sure your foot is turned in and pointing slightly down. Keep your ankle stiff. You swing into the kick with your calf—the part of your leg below the knee.

Practice this skill against the wall as you did with the shooting exercises. Remember, this pass, like the inside-the-foot pass, is meant for accuracy, not power.

THE INSTEP DRIVE

This is used when you're trying to kick a ball with power and for distance. It's called an instep drive because you kick the ball with your instep, the upper side of your foot where the laces are—the hardest part of the foot. To get the ball where you want it to go, be sure that your instep hits the center of the ball. If you hit it on the side, the ball is going to curve away. If you hit it too low, the ball will pop up high but will not go very far.

RECEIVING THE BALL

If another team player wants to pass the ball to you because she can't get a clear shot at the goal, or is surrounded by players from the other team, you need to be in an open position to receive the ball. You can't be right behind a player from the other team, or she'll intercept the pass or steal the ball from you. You also don't want to get too close to the player who's trying to pass the ball—you and your teammate have to open up enough room to get the ball away from the other team. You have to be quick; watch your teammate but stay aware of where the other players are at the same time and move to an open space.

When you're receiving a ball that is airborne, "catch" it lightly with your foot as though it was an egg that might break. Allow your foot to stop the ball's progress and guide it gently to the ground. Your foot should move with the ball as it makes contact. If your foot is rigid and unmoving when the ball hits it, you'll make it bounce too far away from you. You want to get control of it as quickly as possible and move downfield before a player from the other team can steal the ball.

Suppose that the ball is coming toward you on the ground. Bend your knees, with one foot ahead of the other. Receive the ball with the inside of your lead foot. Keep your foot in the same position you would use for an inside-the-foot pass. Remember to keep your ankle locked. Watch the ball come all the way to your foot and "catch" it.

You and a friend can practice passing and receiving with each other. Make sure that you practice receiving with both feet until you don't have to think about which foot you're using. In a game situation, you will not always be able to position yourself to receive a ball with the foot you feel most comfortable with. If you find that you're using only one foot to receive the ball, force yourself to use the other until it feels more natural.

TENDING GOAL

A goalkeeper needs to know some additional skills that are related to her special position on the team. Remember, if you're a goalkeeper, you're the only player who can use your hands. Your main job is to keep the other team from scoring goals. This means being ready to catch the ball, whether it's in the air or rolling on the ground. Practice catching a soccer ball rolled and thrown at you from all angles and heights and at all speeds. Also practice keeping your body in front of the ball as much as you can. That way, if you miss catching the ball, you might still be able to block it with your hands or body and stop a goal from being made.

You also need to practice your diving saves. Not all shots will come right to you. In fact, most players will try to shoot the ball away from you. So you may have to leap in order to stop some balls from entering the net.

You may have seen other goalkeepers perform such saves, or watched the same thing being done by infield players in baseball—dramatically diving onto their sides, parallel to the

The goalie not only has to be quick to move, she also has to anticipate where the shooter might aim and then begin to move in that direction.

ground, to snag line drives. If the ball is aimed away from you and comes so quickly that you can't catch it from where you stand, you have to be ready to dive and catch it, or at least knock it away from the goal. You do this by lunging at the ball, feet off the ground and arms outstretched. If you catch the ball, hug it to you as you land. If you can't get close enough to the ball to wrap your hands around it or trap it in your arms, punch it away from the goal.

Diving saves aren't easy. None of us really likes throwing ourselves down onto the hard ground. But if you learn how to dive correctly, it shouldn't hurt. At first, you should just try short dives so that you can get used to hitting the ground. Then try longer dives with more power behind them. Finally, try a full, lunging dive as someone throws a ball well away from you. See how often you can catch it.

Once you have caught or grabbed the ball, you have to know how to get rid of it. You have only six seconds to put the ball back in play. You can throw the ball back in. You can also punt it back in. A punt means dropping the ball toward your foot and kicking it with your instep to get it to go as high and far down the field—and away from your goal—as possible.

Don't worry if you don't get this right at first. The more you practice punting, the better you'll get at it. Try to get in some practice punts as well as some practice dives and throws every day.

USING YOUR HEAD

Heading the ball is a way to shoot or pass a ball that's in the air rather than on the ground. The trick is to hit the ball with your forehead at your hairline (where your hair meets your forehead). It's important to keep your eyes open and on the ball so that you hit the ball rather than letting the ball hit you.

Heading the ball is a good way to "catch" a high pass or to move the ball when you can't use your feet. The hardest part is getting over the fear of using your head.

It's not easy to overcome the natural fear of having something flying toward your head. But if you practice often enough, you'll be able to overcome that fear. Try hanging a soccer ball by a rope from a tree, and then practice leaping up to hit the ball with your forehead. Then move on to tossing a ball up into the air and hitting it with your forehead. You can start with something lighter than a soccer ball, such as an inflatable or foam ball, until you get used to heading.

CHAPTER FOUR

FACING YOUR OPPONENTS

Competition is the name of the game in soccer. You may be perfectly happy just playing soccer with your friends. There's nothing wrong with simply having fun. But what if you decide you want to be part of a team that competes? Schools and YWCAs are good places to start looking for instruction and a team on which to play. But what sort of teams are there to choose from?

Soccer players up to eighteen years old are usually ranked according to age. The youngest division, U-6, is made up of children as young as four and a half and as old as five. The next jump is to U-8, for children six to seven. Then comes U-10, for children eight to nine. After that is U-12, for ages ten to eleven, then U-14, for ages twelve to thirteen. Last is U-16, for ages fourteen to fifteen, and U-19, for ages sixteen through eighteen. After age eighteen, a player is classified as an adult and is eligible to join an adult league

Japan's players celebrate winning the FIFA Women's World Cup against the US team in 2011. The US team went on to win the Women's World Cup against Japan in 2015.

Once you enter middle school or junior high, you can also join your school team.

Before you can join a team, you sometimes have to try out for it. Some soccer clubs require a new tryout every season. High school soccer seasons start off with tryouts, too. Maybe you don't like tests, but there are a few ways to make tryouts easier on yourself. Start off on the right foot by being on time. Show up wearing clean soccer gear. Be sure you're in good shape. The coaches may be looking for talented or experienced players, but they are even more interested in finding a good group of girls who really want to play soccer, are willing to work hard, and can play together cooperatively as a team.

SOCCER SUPERSTAR ALEX MORGAN

Alex Morgan, a forward for the Portland Thorns FC of the National Women's Soccer League, was born July 2, 1989. She is one of the brightest soccer stars today. Morgan was the number one overall in the 2011 WPS Draft by the Western New York Flash and in 2015, competed in the FIFA Women's World Cup. She is also a *New York Times* best-selling children's book author, having written *The Kicks*, a series of books about four soccer players. In 2014, Amazon Studios greenlighted, or approved, turning *The Kicks* into a television comedy show.

Don't worry about what position you'll be playing on a team. The most important skill you can have as a soccer player is versatility, which means being able to play more than one position. The more you can do as a soccer player, the more likely you are to win a place on the team and become a valuable member.

But whatever happens during your tryout, remember that it's not you who is being accepted or rejected. It's your soccer skills. And those are, after all, only a small part of who you are as a person. If you do make a team on the first attempt, that's great.

WHEN PARENTS ARE THE PROBLEM

There's one problem with competing that has nothing to do with the game itself, and that is some players' parents. They don't really mean to, but they can get carried away—yelling insults at the other team or the coach, loudly criticizing their daughters' coach or teammates, or blaming their own daughters for not playing better. Instead of getting into a fight with your parents by saying "Don't yell at the coach" or "Who's playing this game, me or you?" try being positive. Suggest to your parents what they can do to be helpful.

Instead of yelling insults, they could shout encouragement to your team. Maybe they could also volunteer to bring refreshments or help maintain the field. Above all, you and your parents should always remember that the point of playing a game is to have fun. Winning is meaningless if the game isn't enjoyable.

SOCCER FOR SUCCESS

The members of the United States women's national team are not

Team USA poses for a group photo at the 2012 Summer Olympics, where they won their fourth Olympic Gold Medal against Japan at Wembley Stadium, London.

Crystal Dunn of Team USA gets ready to shoot the ball during the FIFA U-20 Women's World Cup in Hiroshima, Japan, in 2012.

only champions on the field, they are champions at home, too. Many of the players provide soccer clinics and talks to encourage girls to play soccer and succeed. They also participate in programs such as Smoke Free Soccer, an international public health campaign.

The message the team delivers to girls is: "Play soccer, live a healthy lifestyle—and don't smoke." The team has made many public appearances for the program, and Smoke Free Soccer posters picturing them in action have been distributed at soccer games, at schools, and to community recreation leagues. A poster of women's soccer players states, "U.S. women rule with fire, not smoke."

In general, you should be very proud of yourself because you're striving for success. If you don't make the team the first time you try out, don't worry. You can always work to improve your skills. Keep practicing, play soccer with friends, and try out again. No matter what, soccer should always be fun for you.

There are also several soccer federations, many of which take young players as members, including the American Youth Soccer Organization (AYSO), which is a national support and training center for young soccer players. Its slogan is "Everyone plays," and it means it. It even has programs for players with physical or mental disabilities. The United States Soccer Federation (USSF) supports soccer all over the world and is responsible for developing US national teams in the United States at all different age levels, as well as building the US Olympic team.

CHAPTER FIVE

PLAY SMART

Play like a girl! That's right. Show the boys that you can beat them at a sport that has always been predominantly male. How can you make sure that you and the other members of your team are treated the same way as boys' soccer teams? Insist on it. Don't let anyone call you "girl soccer players." You're "soccer players," period. Some referees are softer on girls' teams—or sometimes stricter—than they would be on teams made up of boys. If you think that a referee is being unfair to your team, tell your coach. But remember that if you want equality on the sports field, you also have to accept that a good coach won't make it easier for you "because you're a girl."

The key to success in soccer is having respect for your teammates as well as your opponents. Collaboration and healthy competition are what the game is all about.

YOU AND YOUR TEAM

Everyone has off days, those times when nothing goes right and you start snapping at your friends or family members. This can happen among teammates, too. We're all human, and humans sometimes get jealous of each other or think that they are better than or not as good as someone else.

These problems can start tearing a team apart. What can you, as a team member, do? Remember, first of all, that you can't change another person. But you can make things easier for everyone.

Greet other team members with a smile and call them by name. Try complimenting another girl when she makes a good play instead of criticizing her if she does something wrong. It's the coach's job, not yours, to correct a player's mistake. Don't gossip or spread rumors about another player. Politely refuse to listen if someone else tries to gossip to you. You may not solve all the team's problems, but at least you'll make things more pleasant for everyone—and for yourself, too.

LEARNING ABOUT YOURSELF

What if the problem isn't with your team, but with you? It was fine when you were playing against your friends. Then it was all just for fun. You knew them and knew they weren't going to hurt you.

But what happens when you realize you're going into competition against girls you don't know? As you watch the opposing team warm up, you may find yourself thinking, "They're better players than we are." That type of thinking can defeat you even before the game begins. So if you do start thinking negative thoughts, use reason to get rid of fear. Simply ask yourself, "How do I know they are better?" Since you haven't seen them play yet, the only answer is, "I don't!"

You may also find yourself worrying that the other team's players are bigger or stronger. That's when you should start being logical again. If they really are bigger, think, "Smaller is faster. I can run rings around them." If they look stronger, think, "So what? This is soccer, not weight lifting! Skills, not brute strength, win soccer games."

You may also be worried about making mistakes in front of your teammates, coach, parents, or even the other team. Mistakes are a fact of life; we all make them on a daily basis. The important thing is that you continue to play the game instead of getting embarrassed or mad at yourself. If you make a mistake during practice, why worry? Practice is just that, a time for improving your skills, making mistakes, and correcting them. But if you're worried before a game, remind yourself that no one is perfect. Even the best players in the world make mistakes. Just play the game, and enjoy yourself. Anxiety can often make you tense up and flub a play you've practiced a thousand times. The more fun you are having, the more loose you will be and therefore less likely to make a mistake. And if you're having fun, you won't care very much about the few minor mistakes you might make.

This kind of anxiety isn't logical, but it is very common and perfectly normal. It has a name: stage fright, the fear of playing or performing in public. Once you do get out there and start playing, there won't be any time for fear. And there won't be any need for it either—you'll be having too much fun. Right after the first kickoff, your nervousness will disappear, and you'll get lost in the game.

THE NEW WORLD OF SOCCER

As a soccer player, or someone who is about to become a soccer player, you've picked a good time to be in the sport. Soccer is becoming more and more popular, both in the United States and in Canada. More and more teams are springing up all the time—both

Team USA has won numerous Olympic medals and World Cup championships. Here, members of the team celebrate their 2015 FIFA Women's World Cup victory.

all girl teams and teams with both boys and girls.

There is plenty of girls' competition at the high school and college level. Today, because of Title IX, it is extremely rare for a high school or college not to have a women's soccer program. There are now more soccer scholarships available than ever before for women going to college.

You don't have to stop playing soccer after you graduate from high school or college either. The US women's national team and the US women's Olympic team are made up of women in their twenties and thirties. Women's soccer has become a well-established part of the Olympic Games. The FIFA Women's World Cup held it's seventh tournament in 2015, won by Team USA.

And without question, whether you want to play just for fun, on a school team, in an amateur league, or as a professional, the time

LIVING LEGEND: MICHELLE AKERS

One of the reasons for the growing popularity of women's soccer has to be Michelle Akers. She was the first women's soccer player to gain worldwide fame.

Akers started her career in college, at the University of Central Florida, where she was an NCAA 1st Team All-American from 1984 to 1989. She was ESPN Athlete of the Year in 1985 and a winner of the Hermann Trophy in 1988. In 1991, she played in the World Cup, scoring ten goals—more than anyone else in the competition—as she helped the US team to victory. She was named the Federation Internationale de Football Association (FIFA) World Champion. (FIFA is the world soccer organization.) She is a member of the National Soccer Hall of Fame and FIFA's Women's Player of the Century.

Akers was also active in working off of the soccer field, becoming a role model for many young girls and helping to put women's soccer into the limelight. In addition, Akers served as an ambassador for the sport by trying to generate excitement and interest in soccer at many events around the country. She has also written books and articles, including *The Game and the Glory*.

No match has ever been won without support and respect between teammates. Cheer your teammates on and you'll be sure to score that goal.

is right for you to play soccer.

RESPECT!

It's important in soccer (or in any sport) to play fairly and to respect your coach, your teammates, your opponents, the referees, and the fans. All these people are at the game for the same reason: to enjoy soccer.

It's important for you to keep your feelings under control during a game and always show respect for your teammates and opponents. Even though you may get angry or frustrated during a game, you must never foul an opponent on purpose. Besides giving the other team a penalty kick, you could injure the other player or yourself. If it is a serious foul, the referee may even kick you out of the game.

Soccer is a friendly game of skill, speed, and strength. Play the game the way it is meant to be played: by following the rules. After a game, be sure to shake hands with your opponents and their coach, as well as with your own team and coach, whether your team won or lost. This shows you are a good sport and that you appreciate everyone's efforts. Some players at the elite level go as far as exchanging their jerseys after a game!

TIMELINE

3000 BC: In Egypt and the Near East, soccerlike games are played as part of religious rituals.

255 BC–AD 220: In China, a game called *tsu chu* is played. It involves kicking balls of animal skin through a net strung between poles.

AD 1600: In what will become the northeastern United States, Native American tribes play a soccerlike game called *pasuckquakkohowog,* meaning "gathering to play ball with the foot."

1820: Several American colleges play football and soccer, but rules are casual and vary from place to place. Players referee themselves.

1827: Freshman and sophomore classes at Harvard begin holding an annual football match played on the first Monday of the new school year. It is nicknamed "Bloody Monday" because of its rough play and rowdy atmosphere.

1862: The first soccer club in America, the Oneidas of Boston, is formed by Gerritt Smith Miller and is undefeated from 1862 to 1865.

1863: In England, where soccerlike games have been played for centuries, the formal rules of soccer are adopted by the newly formed London Football Association.

1869: Princeton University and Rutgers University play the first intercollegiate soccer game. Rutgers wins.

1873: Inspired by the London Football Association's rules verification, players from Princeton, Yale, Columbia, and Rutgers meet in New York to draw up a similar code of rules based on the ones created in London in 1863.

1904: The St. Louis Olympic Games include soccer as an official sport for men.

1914: The USFA, or United States Football Association, now the United States Soccer Federation, joins FIFA, the Federation Internationale de Football Association, the world soccer organization.

1916: The US team plays Norway and Sweden, becoming the first US men's team to play in Europe.

1920: The first women's professional soccer team is formed. Called the Dick, Kerr's ladies soccer team, it outscores male opponents but fails to last.

1930: The first World Cup is held, for male players only.

1941: The NSCAA, the National Soccer Coaches Association of America, is formed.

1959: The first men's college championship tournament is held. St. Louis University defeats Bridgeport University.

1967: The Hermann Trophy is created. It is awarded to the best male college soccer player each year.

1974: The USFA becomes the United States Soccer Federation (USSF).

1975: Brazilian soccer superstar Pelé comes to the United States to play with the New York Cosmos.

1981: The United States under-twenty men's national team competes in the first World Youth Championship.

1987: The new National Soccer Hall of Fame opens in Oneonta, New York.

1991: The United States women's national team captures the first FIFA Women's World Championship. It is the first world title ever won by an American soccer team.

1994: The United States hosts the men's World Cup for the first time.

1995: The United States women's national team attends the women's World Cup in Sweden and finishes third

1996: The United States women's national team wins the gold medal in the first-ever women's soccer event at the Atlanta Olympic Games.

1998: The United States women's national team wins its fifth straight Nike Women's Cup.

1999: The United States hosts the women's World Cup. The US women's national team reclaims the World Cup trophy. The renovated National Soccer Hall of Fame reopens in Oneonta, New York.

2006: Title IX regulations are amended to include single-sex classes or extracurricular activities at the primary or secondary school level.

2010: Soccer in the Streets is represented the United States at the Football for Hope Festival FIFA World Cup.

2011: Soccer in the Streets wins its first ATL Champions League.

2015: Team USA wins the FIFA Women's World Cup against Japan.

GLOSSARY

ASSIST When one player passes the ball to another, who then scores.

AYSO American Youth Soccer Organization, a soccer program with the slogan "Everyone plays."

BENCH The place on the sidelines for player substitutes and the coaches.

CALL A referee's decision.

DEFENDERS The players responsible for helping the goalie stop the other team from scoring.

DRIBBLING Moving the ball with short, controlled touches.

FIFA The Federation Internationale de Football Association, the world soccer organization.

FORWARDS The players whose main job is to get through the other team's defense and score.

FOUL An illegal play.

GOAL Two goalposts connected by a crossbar, placed on the goal line. The term is also used to indicate when the ball goes between the goalposts and scores a point.

GOALKEEPER, GOALIE The only player allowed to use her hands to control the ball. Her job is to stop the other team from scoring.

INSTEP The top of the foot where the laces of your shoe are.

LINESPEOPLE Assistant referees, two for each game, who stand on the sidelines.

MIDFIELDERS The players between the forwards and defenders, who play both offense and defense during a game.

REFEREE The man or woman who watches the game to be sure all the laws of soccer are obeyed.

SEVER'S DISEASE A common and temporary problem associated with adolescent growth. Sever's disease is damage to the heel resulting from unequal growth rates of the heel bone and Achilles tendon. The pain can be eased with stretching exercises and properly fitting shoes.

SHOT Kicking the ball at the goal in an attempt to score.

USSF United States Soccer Federation, the official agency of US soccer.

USYSA United States Youth Soccer Association, the youth branch of the USSF.

WORLD CUP The FIFA World Cup, an international soccer competition held once every four years.

FOR MORE INFORMATION

American Youth Soccer Organization
19750 S. Vermont Avenue, Suite 200
Torrance, CA 90502
(800) USA-AYSO (800-872-2976)
Web site: http://www.ayso.org
Consisting of over fifty thousand teams and five hundred thou-
    sand players nationwide, AYSO is one of the leading youth
    soccer organizations in the world.

Canadian Soccer Association
237 Metcalfe Street
Ottawa, ON K2P 1R2
Canada
(613) 237-7678
Web site: http://www.canadasoccer.com
The Canadian Soccer Association (Canada Soccer) is the
    official governing body for soccer in Canada.

Canadian Soccer League
66 Pennsylvania Avenue
Concord, ON L4K 3V9
Canada
(905) 564-2297
Website: www.canadiansoccerleague.ca
The Canadian Soccer League (CSL) is long-standing and is the
    highest level league in Canada.

FIFA (Fédération Internationale de Football Association)
FIFA-Strasse 20,
P.O. Box 8044 Zurich, Switzerland
+41-(0)43 222 7777
Website: www.fifa.com
The Fédération Internationale de Football Association (FIFA) is
    an association governed by Swiss law founded in 1904 and
    whose mission is the constant improvement of football.

United States Soccer Federation (USSF)
1801 South Prairie Avenue
Chicago, IL 60616
(312) 808-1300
Web site: http://www.ussoccer.com
United States Soccer Federation is the governing body of
    soccer in all its forms in the United States.

United States Youth Soccer
9220 World Cup Way
Frisco, TX 75033
(800) 4SOCCER (1-800-476-2237)
Web site: http://www.usysa.org
US Youth Soccer is the largest member of the United States
    Soccer Federation, the governing body for soccer in the
    United States.

US Department of Education
400 Maryland Avenue SW
Washington, D.C. 20202
800-USA-LEARN (1-800-872-5327)
Website: www.ed.gov
The US Department of Education's mission is to promote student achievement and preparation for global competitiveness by fostering educational excellence and ensuring equal access.

Women's Sports Foundation
Newbridge Avenue
East Meadow, NY 11554
(516) 542-4700
Website: http://www.womenssportsfoundation.org
Founded in 1974 by tennis legend Billie Jean King, the Women's Sports Foundation is dedicated to advancing the lives of girls and women through sports and physical activity.

WEBSITES

Because of the changing nature of Internet links, Rosen Publishing has developed an online list of websites related to the subject of this book. This site is updated regularly. Please use this link to access the list:

http://www.rosenlinks.com/IX/Soccer

FOR FURTHER READING

Doeden, Matt. *The World's Greatest Soccer Players.* Mankato, MN: Capstone, 2010.

Downing, Erin. *For Soccer-crazy Girls Only.* New York, NY: Feiwel & Friends, 2014.

Etoe, Catherine, Jen O'Neill, and Natalia Sollohub. *FIFA Women's World Cup Canada, 2015: The Official Book.* New York, NY: Abbeville, 2015.

Goldblatt, David, and Johnny Acton. *The Soccer Book: The Sport, the Teams, the Tactics, the Cups.* New York, NY: DK, 2014.

Hoena, B. A., and Omar Gonzalez. *Everything Soccer.* New York, NY: National Geographic Children's, 2014.

Howard, Tim, and Ali Benjamin. *The Keeper: The Unguarded Story of Tim Howard.* New York, NY: HarperCollins, 2015.

Jökulsson, Illugi. *Alex Morgan.* New York, NY: Abbeville Kids, 2015.

Radnedge, Keir. *World Soccer Records 2015.* New York, NY: Carlton, 2015.

INDEX

ABOUT THE AUTHORS

Nicholas Faulkner is a writer living in New Jersey.

Josepha Sherman is a fantasy, science fiction, and Star Trek novelist, a professional folklorist, and an editor with almost forty books currently in print.

PHOTO CREDITS

Cover Lopolo/Shutterstock.com; p. 5 Julian Finney/FIFA/Getty Images; pp. 8-9 Dariusz Paciorek/E+/Getty Images; pp. 10-11 © AP Images; p. 14 Erik Isakson/Blend Images/Getty Images; pp. 16-17 Andresr/Shutterstock.com; p. 19 Le Do/iStock/Thinkstock; p. 21 Enrico Calderoni/Getty Images; pp. 24-25 Jules Frazier/Photodisc/Getty Images; p. 27 Brad Thompson/Shutterstock.com; p. 28 moodboard/Cultura/Getty Images; p. 31 strickke/E+/Getty Images; pp. 34-35 Barry Austin/Photodisc/Thinkstock; p. 37 © iStockphoto.com/isitsharp; p. 39 Christof Stache/AFP/Getty Images; p. 41 Al Tielemans/Sports Illustrated/Getty Images; p. 42 Kiyoshi Ota/FIFA/Getty Images; p. 45 Thomas Barwick/Iconica/Getty Images; p. 48 Franck Fife/AFP/Getty Images; pp. 50-51 Image Source/Getty Images; cover and interior pages graphic elements vector illustration/Shutterstock.com.
Designer: Nicole Russo; Editor: Nicholas Croce; Photo Researcher: Karen Huang